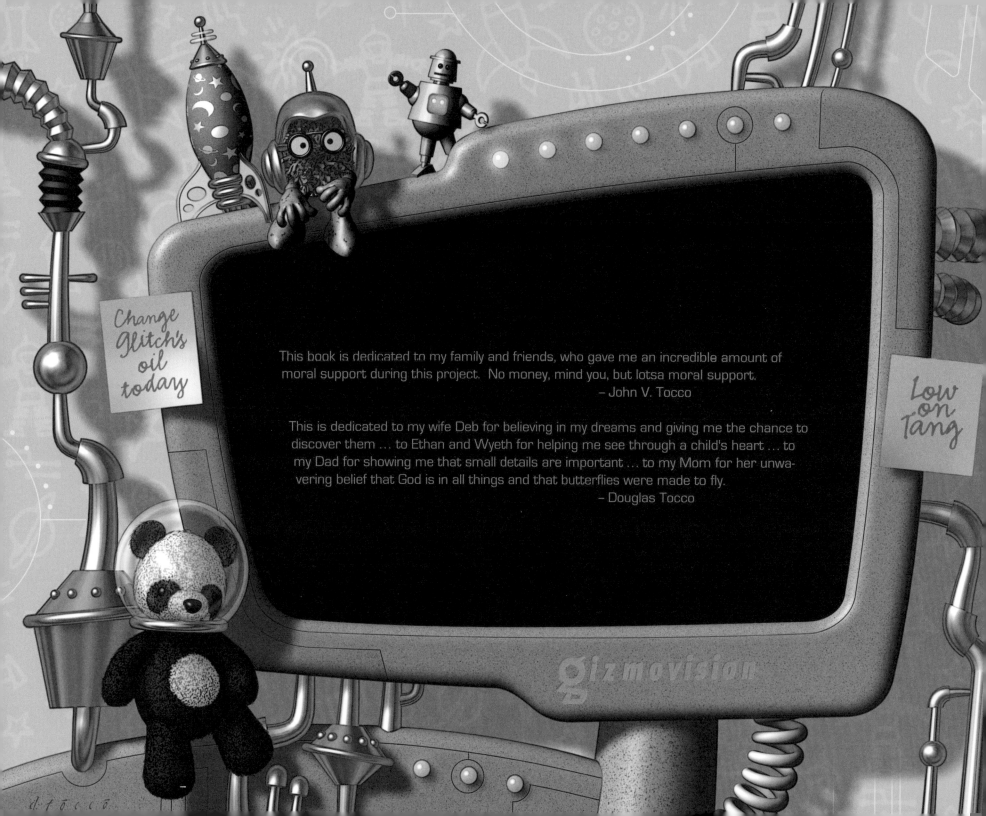

Change Glitch's oil today

Low on Tang

This book is dedicated to my family and friends, who gave me an incredible amount of moral support during this project. No money, mind you, but lotsa moral support.
– John V. Tocco

This is dedicated to my wife Deb for believing in my dreams and giving me the chance to discover them … to Ethan and Wyeth for helping me see through a child's heart … to my Dad for showing me that small details are important … to my Mom for her unwavering belief that God is in all things and that butterflies were made to fly.
– Douglas Tocco

gizmovision

MEET THE GIZMOS

words by
John V. Tocco

Favorite™
Uncle
Books

pictures by
Douglas Tocco

www.FavoriteUncleBooks.com
www.Gizmovision.com

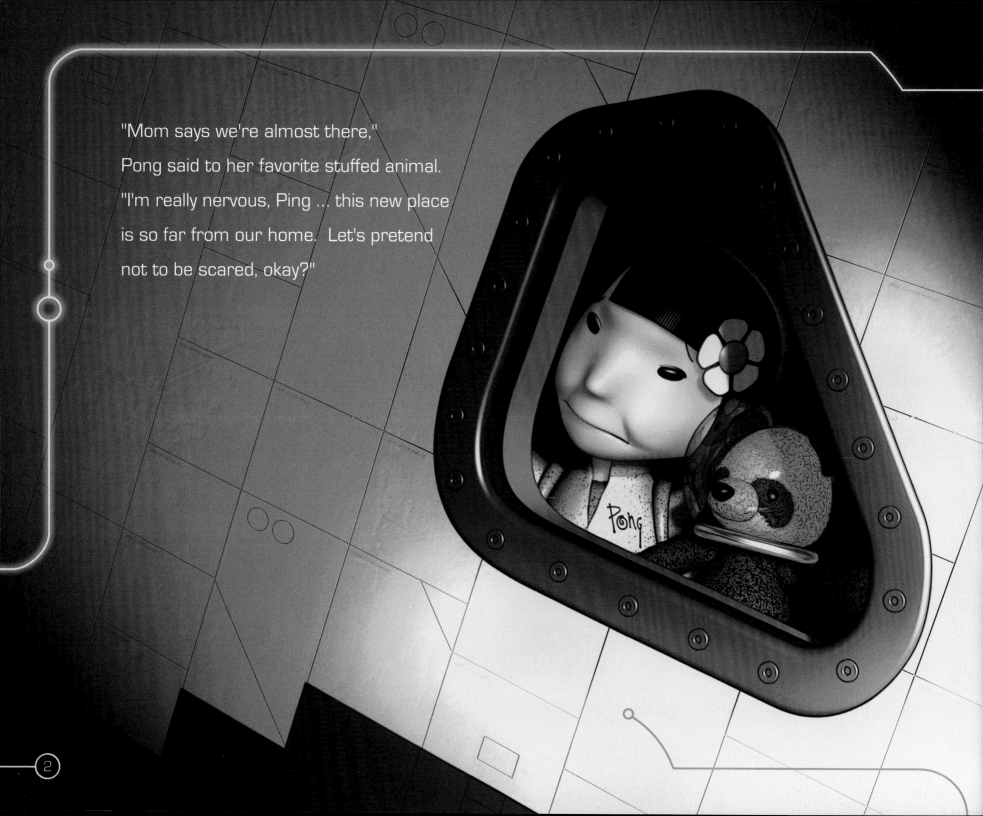

"Mom says we're almost there,"
Pong said to her favorite stuffed animal.
"I'm really nervous, Ping ... this new place
is so far from our home. Let's pretend
not to be scared, okay?"

Meanwhile...

"Hustle up, guys! She's almost here!" called Angela.

"Roger, Cap'n Angie," Yuri replied.

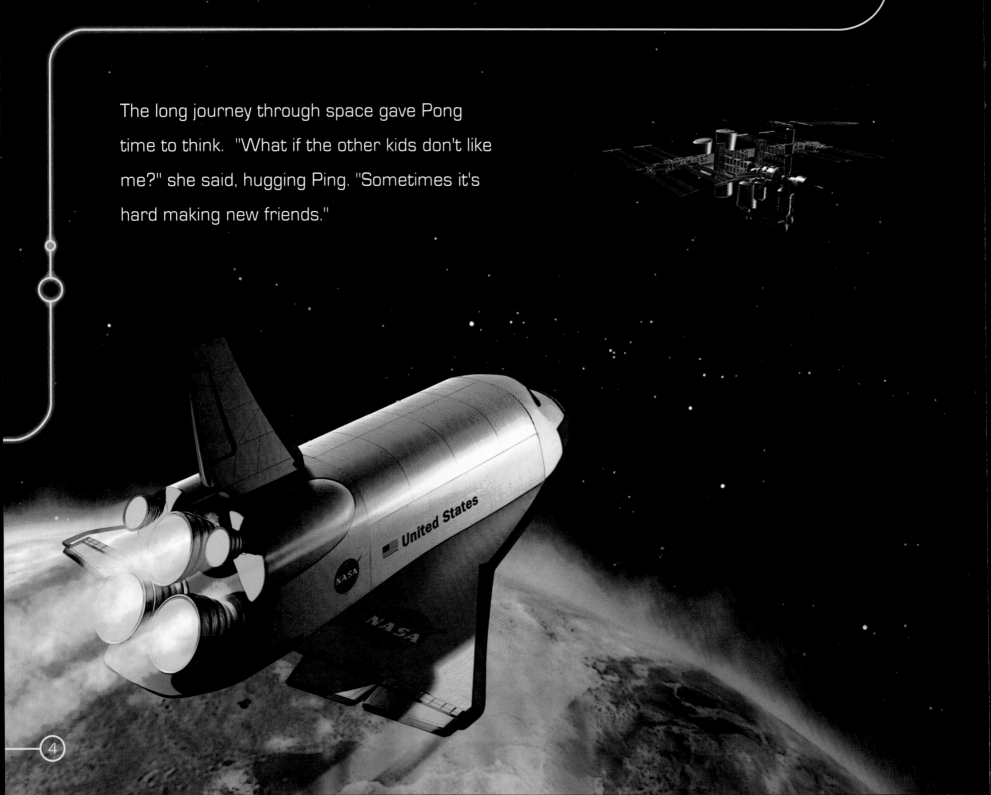

The long journey through space gave Pong time to think. "What if the other kids don't like me?" she said, hugging Ping. "Sometimes it's hard making new friends."

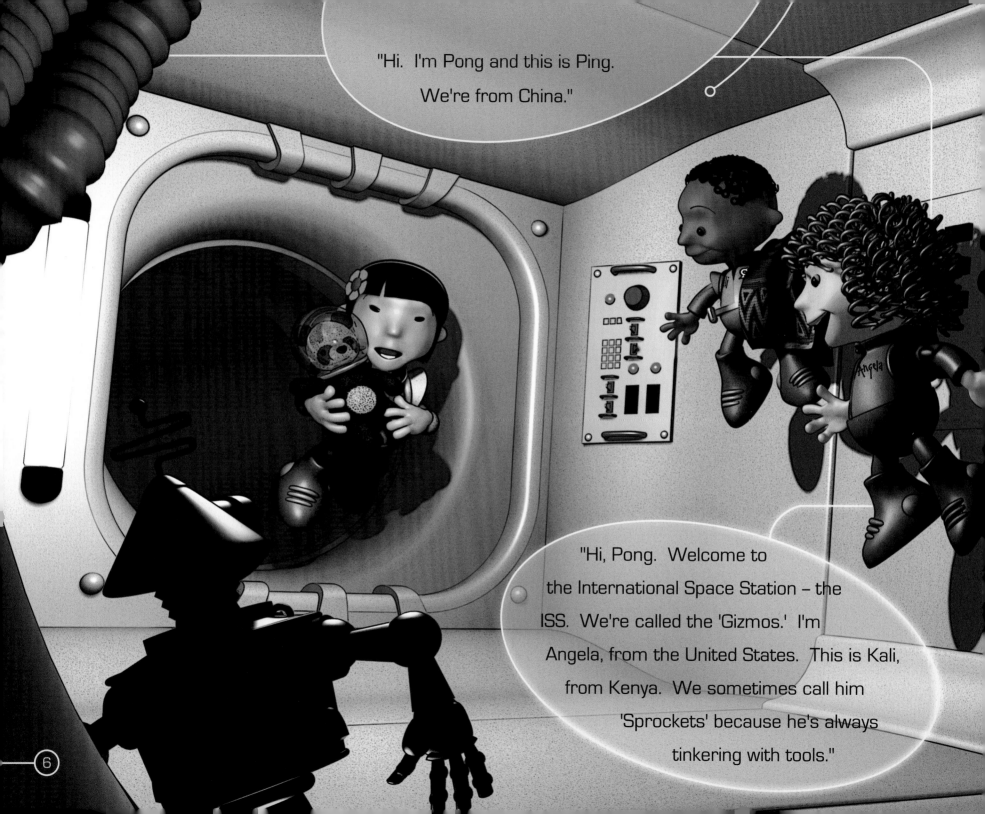

"I'm Yuri, from Russia, and this is our Gizbot, Glitch. He's from 'Parts Unknown.'"

"What's a 'Gizmo?'" asked Pong.

"Like your mom and dad, our parents are crewmembers of the ISS," Kali explained. "They nicknamed us 'Gizmos' 'cause we like to build things out of spare space parts."

"Things like *me*," said Glitch, in his monotone mechanical voice. "Greetings, Miss Pong."

"Hi, Glitch. That's a beautiful sign the Gizmos made for me. But there's no air in space. How did they hold their breath for so long?"

Glitch's gears whirled and lights blinked. "If you wear a space suit like Gizmo Yuri you do not have to hold your breath. His backpack makes air to breathe, and his face shield protects him from space particles."

"Isn't it really cold in space?" Pong asked. "Is Yuri wearing an extra sweater?"

"It does get cold, and sometimes quite hot. But do not worry. The suit keeps the temperature just right."

"How do the Gizmos talk to each other in space, Glitch?"

"Through a communicator, like this." *Beep!* "It is snack time, Yuri."

Beep! "Roger, Glitchster." Yuri's voice crackled over the station speaker.

"The space suits work great, but they're *boring*," Angela said.

Glitch buzzed. "What do you mean, Gizmo Angela?"

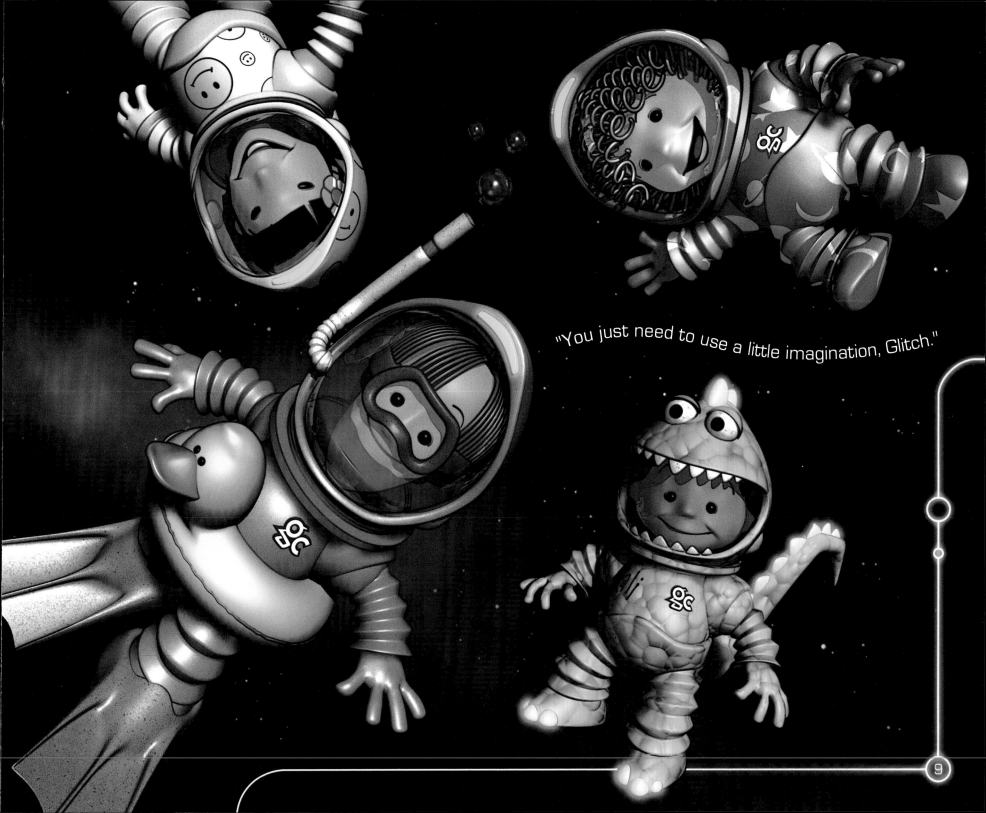

"You just need to use a little imagination, Glitch."

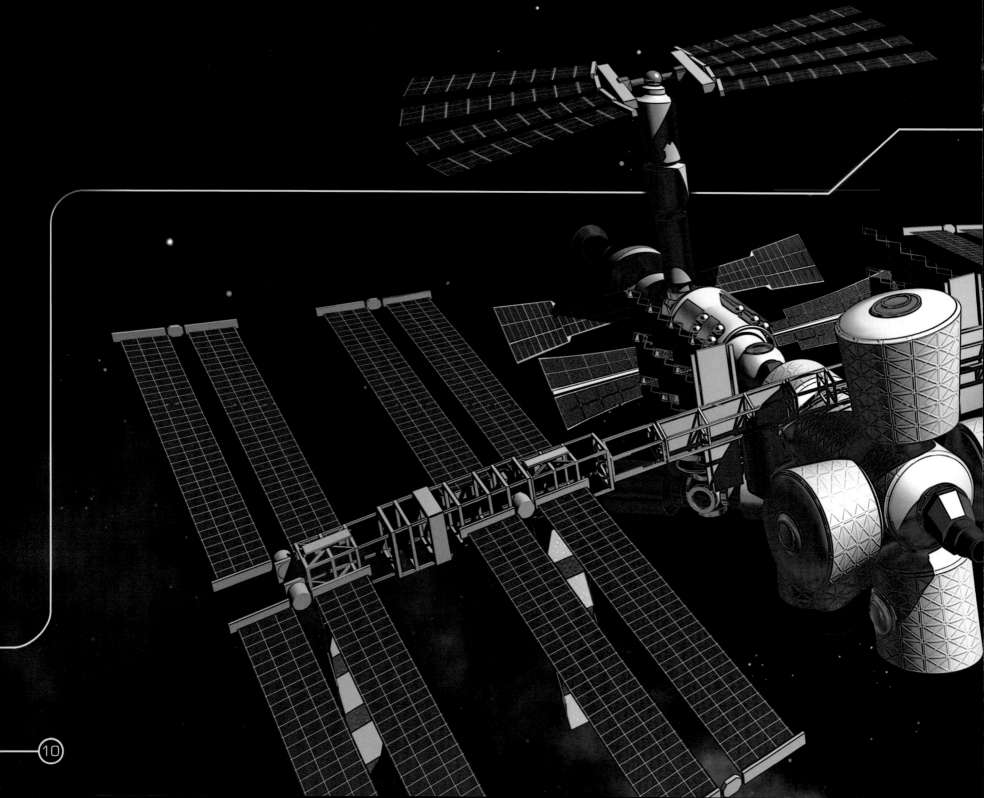

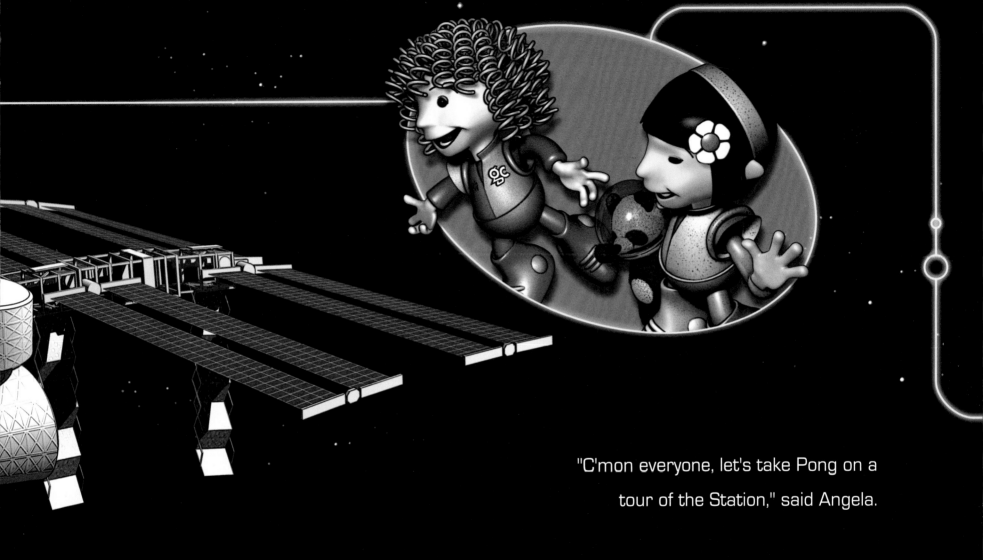

"C'mon everyone, let's take Pong on a tour of the Station," said Angela.

Pong pointed out the window. "What are those things that look like wings, Angela?"

"Those are solar arrays. They collect rays from the sun and turn them into electricity to power the Station."

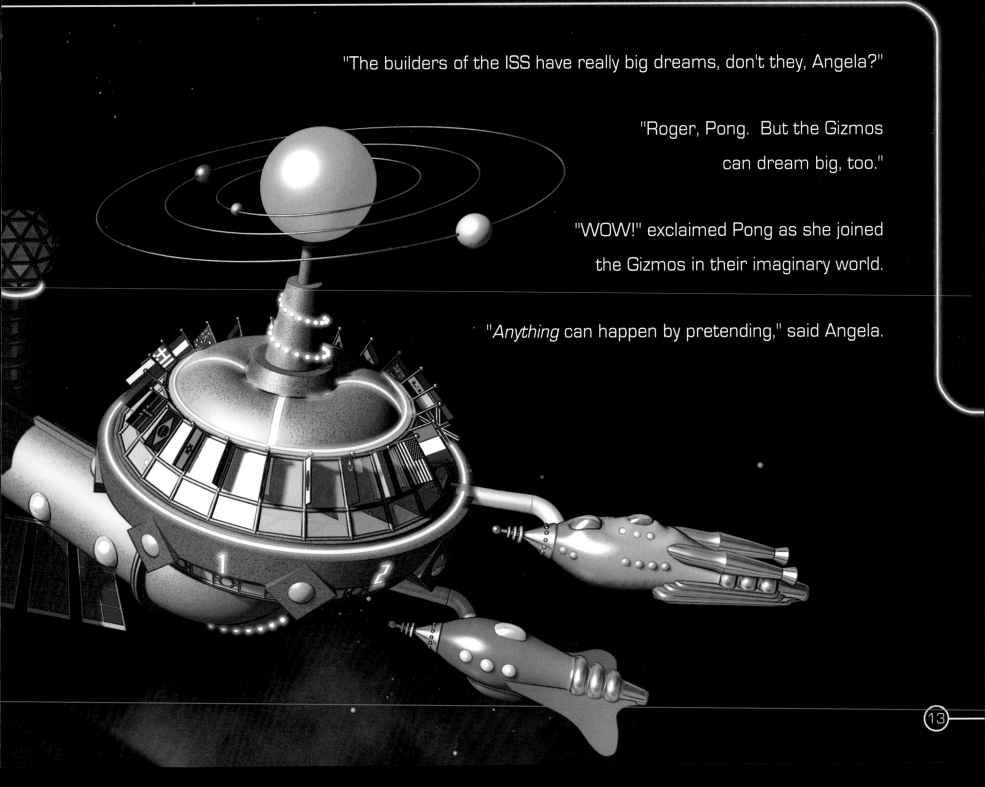

"The builders of the ISS have really big dreams, don't they, Angela?"

"Roger, Pong. But the Gizmos can dream big, too."

"WOW!" exclaimed Pong as she joined the Gizmos in their imaginary world.

"*Anything* can happen by pretending," said Angela.

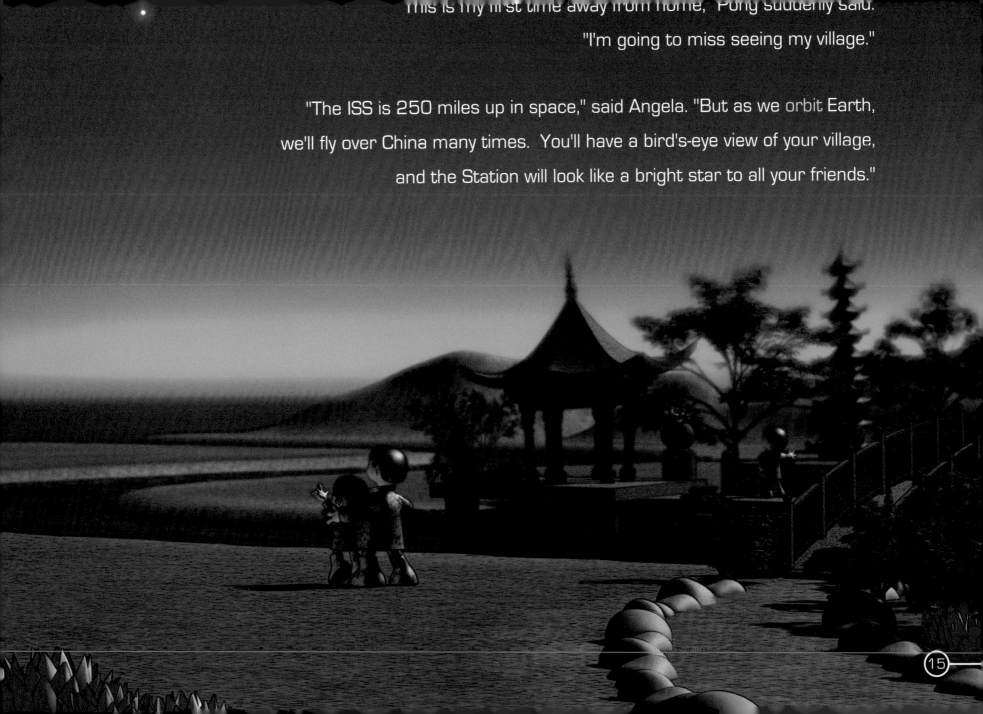

This is my first time away from home," Pony suddenly said.

"I'm going to miss seeing my village."

"The ISS is 250 miles up in space," said Angela. "But as we orbit Earth, we'll fly over China many times. You'll have a bird's-eye view of your village, and the Station will look like a bright star to all your friends."

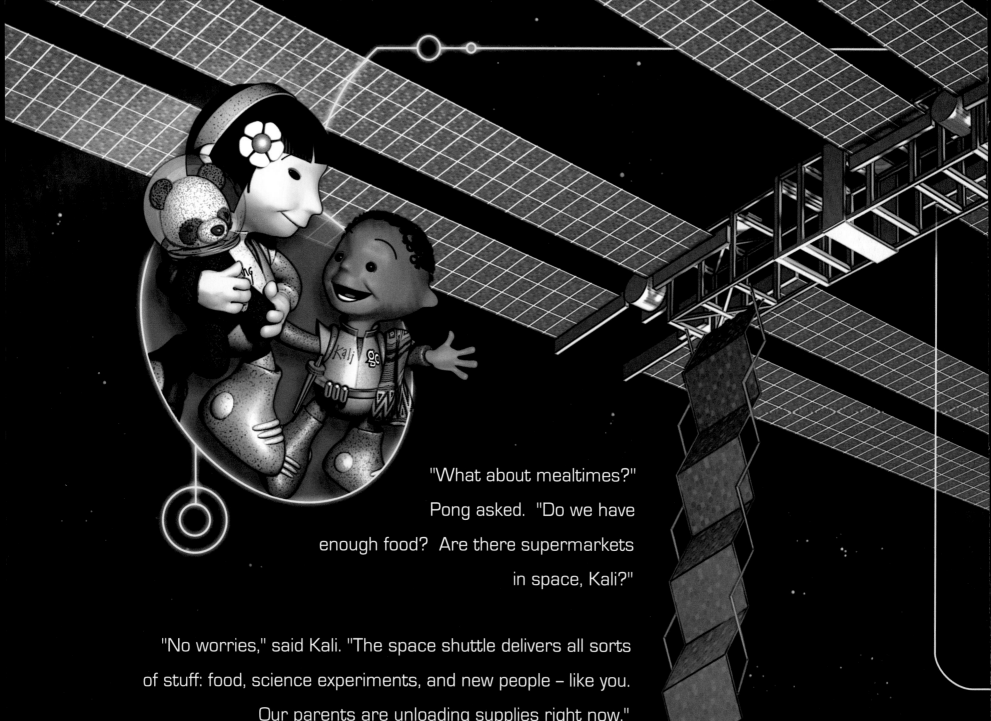

"What about mealtimes?"
Pong asked. "Do we have
enough food? Are there supermarkets
in space, Kali?"

"No worries," said Kali. "The space shuttle delivers all sorts
of stuff: food, science experiments, and new people – like you.
Our parents are unloading supplies right now."

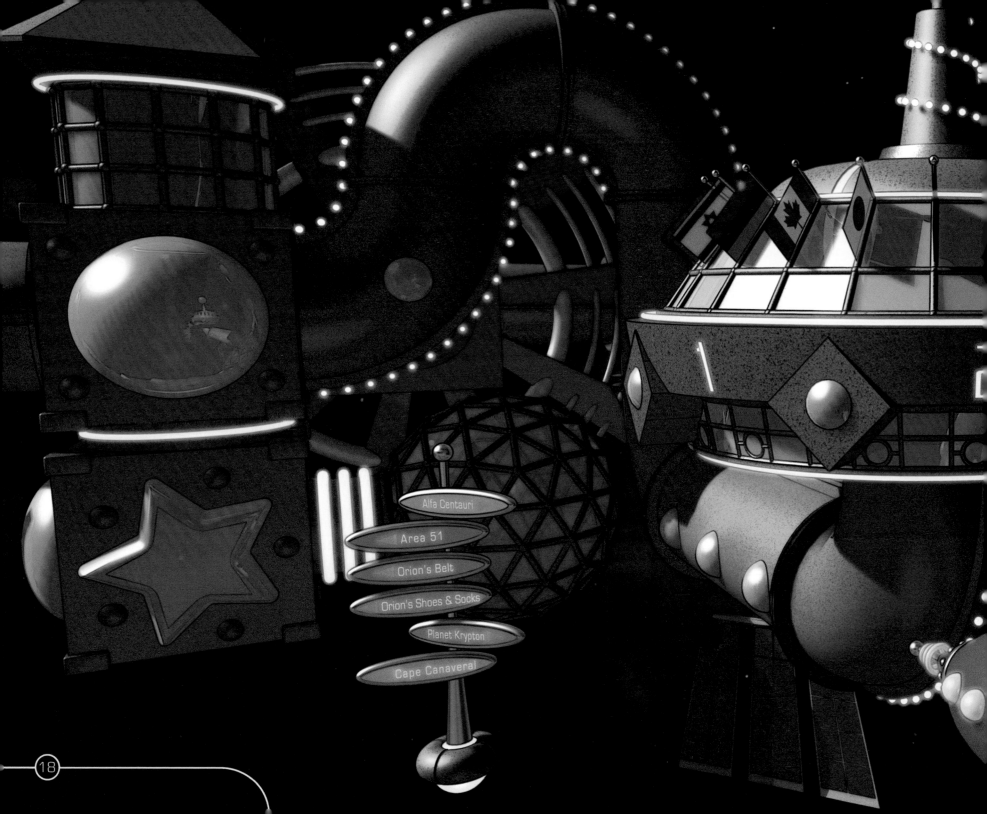

Alfa Centauri

Area 51

Orion's Belt

Orion's Shoes & Socks

Planet Krypton

Cape Canaveral

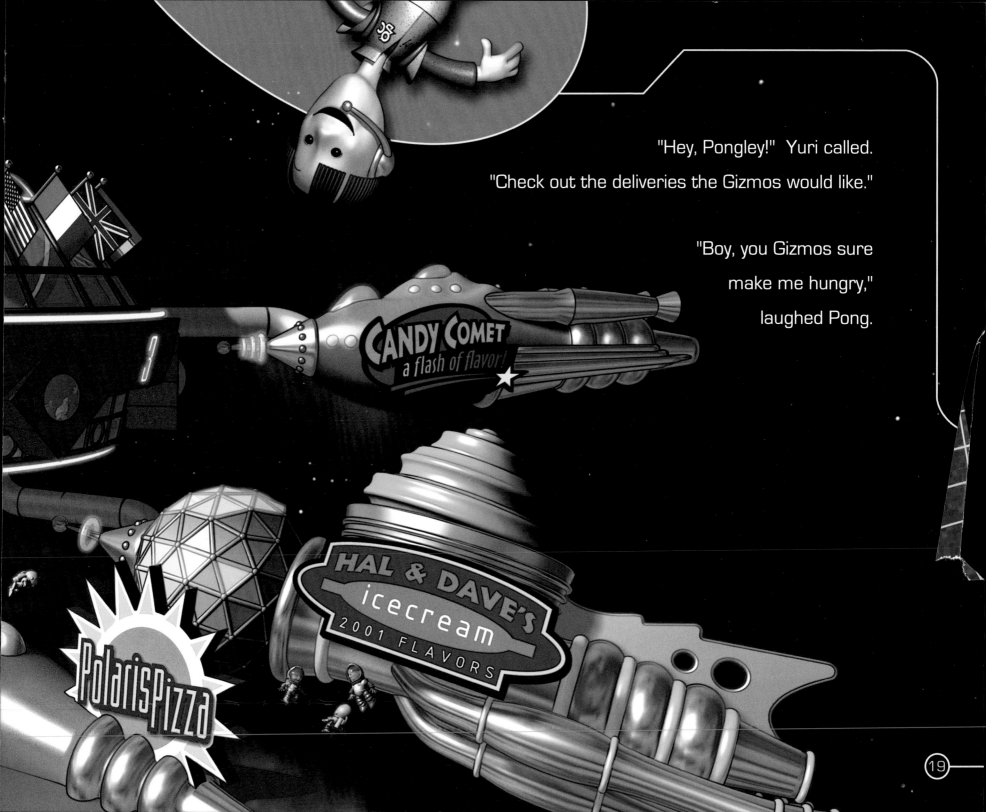

"Hey, Pongley!" Yuri called.
"Check out the deliveries the Gizmos would like."

"Boy, you Gizmos sure
make me hungry,"
laughed Pong.

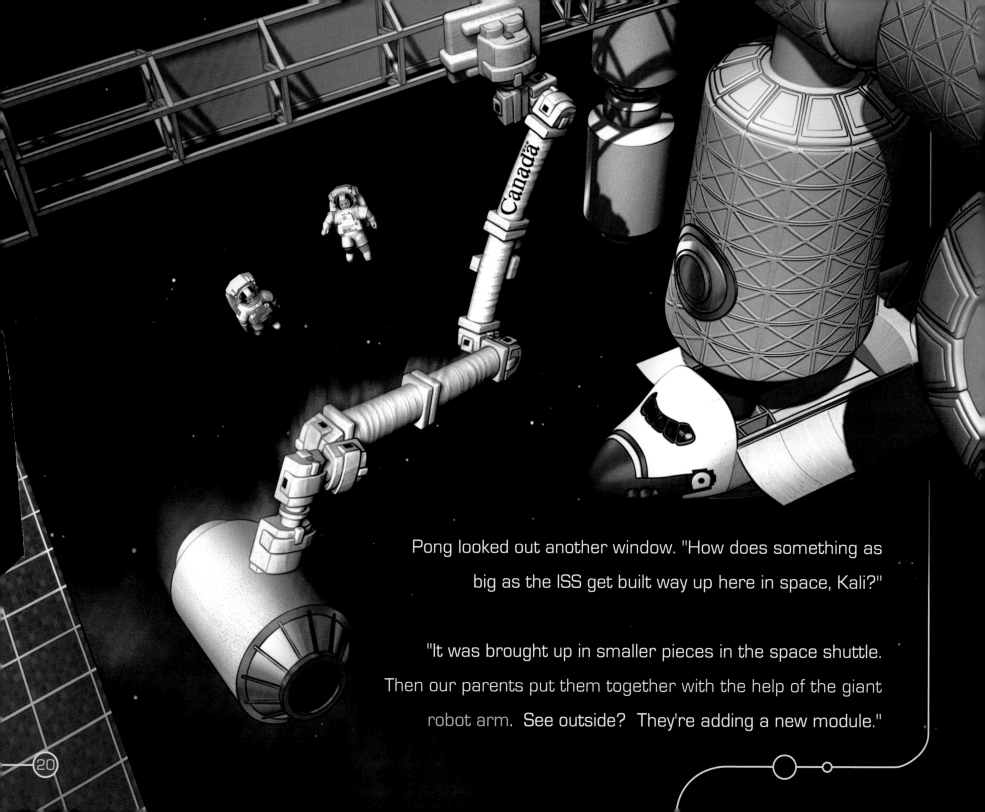

Pong looked out another window. "How does something as big as the ISS get built way up here in space, Kali?"

"It was brought up in smaller pieces in the space shuttle. Then our parents put them together with the help of the giant robot arm. See outside? They're adding a new module."

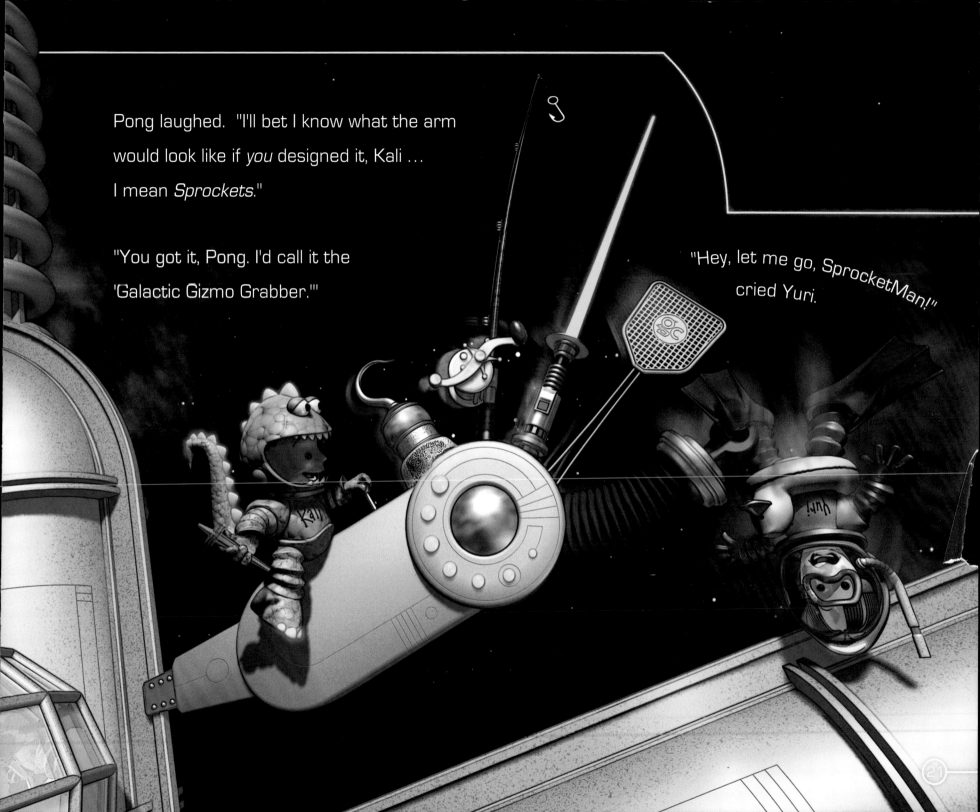

Pong laughed. "I'll bet I know what the arm would look like if *you* designed it, Kali ... I mean *Sprockets*."

"You got it, Pong. I'd call it the 'Galactic Gizmo Grabber.'"

"Hey, let me go, SprocketMan!" cried Yuri.

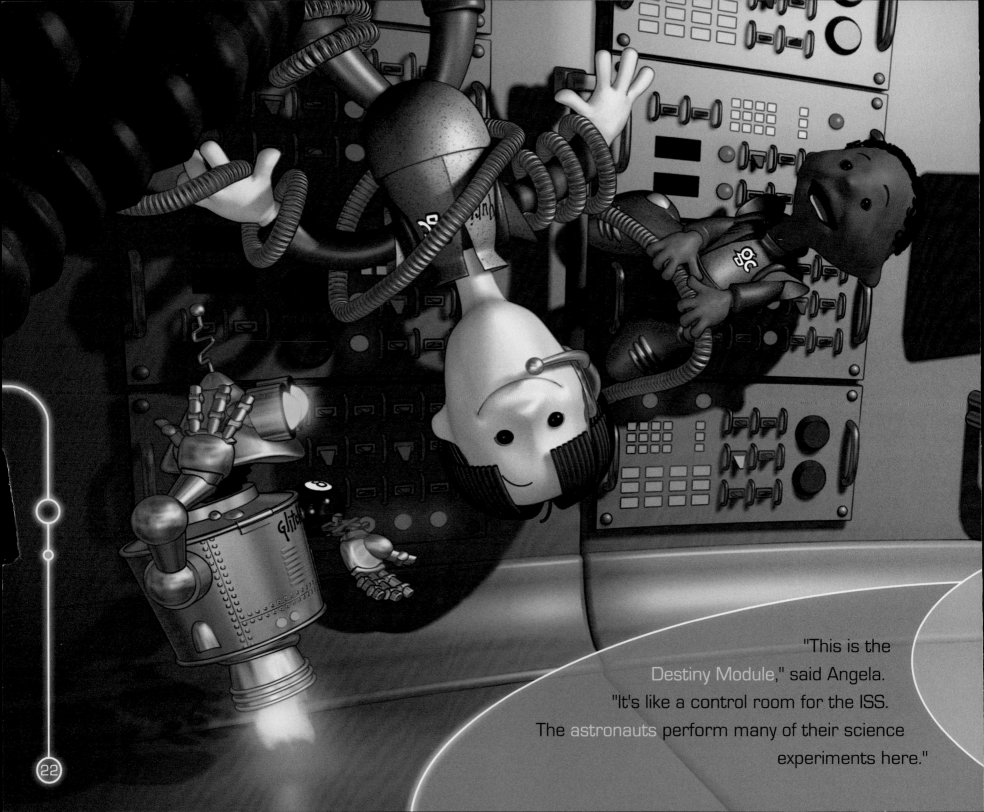

"This is the
Destiny Module," said Angela.
"It's like a control room for the ISS.
The astronauts perform many of their science
experiments here."

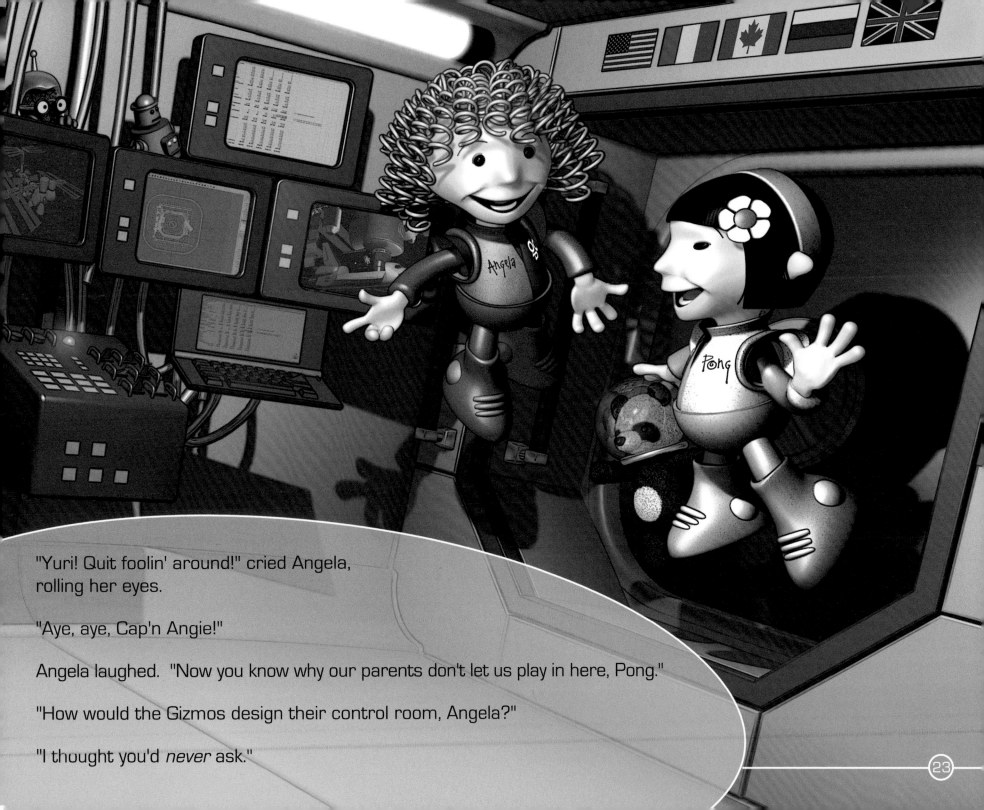

"Yuri! Quit foolin' around!" cried Angela,
rolling her eyes.

"Aye, aye, Cap'n Angie!"

Angela laughed. "Now you know why our parents don't let us play in here, Pong."

"How would the Gizmos design their control room, Angela?"

"I thought you'd *never* ask."

"Welcome to *Gizmo Control*, Pong!"

"Awesome! *That's* what the 'GC' patch on your uniform means. Imagine, a clubhouse full of computers! My dream come true."

"Hey, Ponger!" shouted Yuri. "Want to play some video games?"

"No time to fight invaders," said Angela. "Gotta finish the tour."

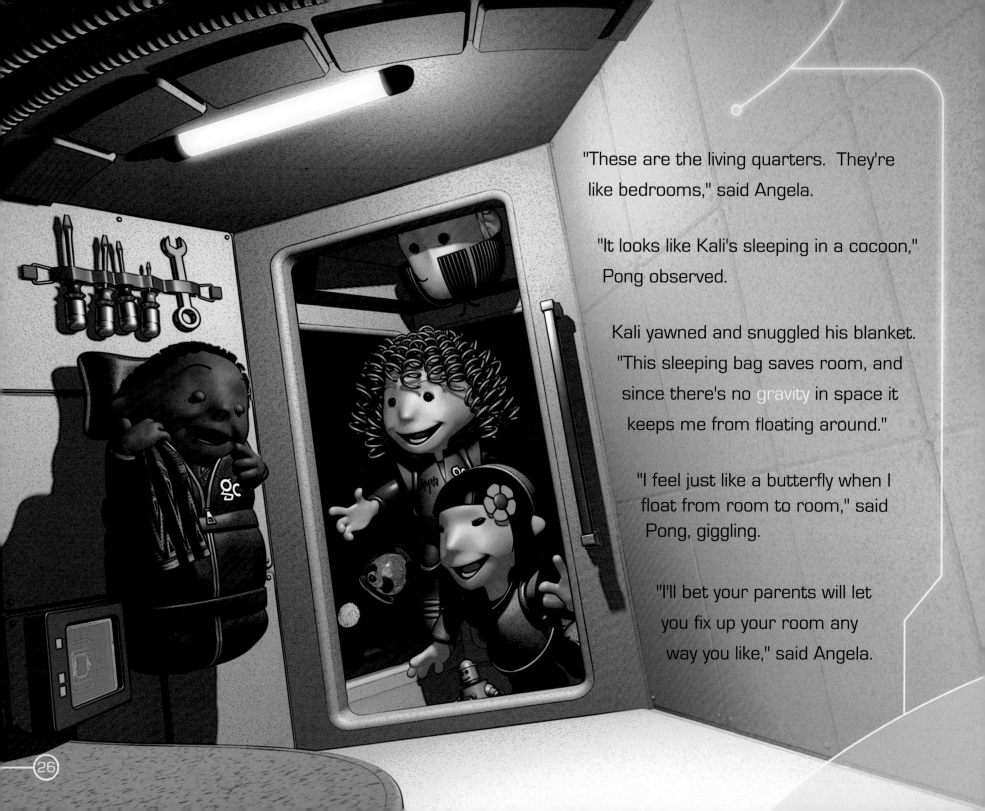

"These are the living quarters. They're like bedrooms," said Angela.

"It looks like Kali's sleeping in a cocoon," Pong observed.

Kali yawned and snuggled his blanket. "This sleeping bag saves room, and since there's no gravity in space it keeps me from floating around."

"I feel just like a butterfly when I float from room to room," said Pong, giggling.

"I'll bet your parents will let you fix up your room any way you like," said Angela.

"Hmm ...
any way I like," said Yuri. "I know
how *my* dream room would look."

"What a great tour," said Pong.

"Gizmo Control is the coolest place in space!

Do you think I could be called a Gizmo someday, too?"

Yuri laughed as he presented her with a Gizmo Control patch. "How about today, PongoPongo? And I didn't forget you, PingPing!"

"Congratulations, Gizmo Pong," added Glitch.

Dear Friends,

I hope you enjoyed your first visit to my new home on the ISS. Sometimes a new place can be scary, but not when I have friends like you and the Gizmos!

Love,

Pong

P.S. Don't forget to wave at me when the ISS flies over your house!

Hi, kids! Thanks for joining us on the International Space Station for our first adventure!

Visit Gizmo Control at www.Gizmovision.com. There are plenty of fun things to do:

○ E-mail your favorite character and tell them all about yourself.

○ Tell us what adventures you'd like to go on if you were a Gizmo.

○ Print out and color pictures of the Gizmos and the ISS.

○ Print out activities like connect the dots, space mazes, and word searches.

○ Let us know if you'd like to become a Gizmo and join Gizmo Control.

Hope to hear from you soon!

the Gizmos

Gizmo Glossary

Here's a list of spacey words that you might want to know more about.

Astronaut – An astronaut is a person who is trained to travel and live in space. Some astronauts are pilots, some are scientists, and some are doctors. *You* may even become an astronaut one day. Yuri's parents, who are from Russia, are called cosmonauts.

Communicator – It is very important that astronauts walking in space keep in contact with the people inside the ISS, people on Earth, and each other. Radio communication equipment is built right into the helmet of the space suit, and includes a microphone and speakers.

Destiny Module – The Destiny Module was built by the United States and brought up to the ISS on the space shuttle Atlantis in February of 2001. It is 28 feet long and 14 feet wide. Destiny is a laboratory where the astronauts perform many different experiments. For example, scientists on Earth are very interested in how plants grow in a weightless environment.

Destiny has a large window that is perfect for viewing Earth. When you go outside to wave at Pong as the ISS flies over, she's probably waving back!

Gravity – Moms and dads aren't the only ones who are attracted to each other. Gravity is the attraction between two objects, like between the Moon and the Earth, or even between *you* and the Earth! The further you travel into space, the weaker gravity gets. On the ISS, astronauts feel almost weightless (they call it micro-gravity). Everything on the Station – computers, equipment, tools – must be tied down or attached with Velcro, or they'll float away.

Orbit – To orbit means to follow a path around something. The Earth revolves around, or orbits, the Sun. The ISS and the Gizmos orbit the Earth.

Robot Arm – The actual robot arm on the ISS has a very fancy name: The Remote Manipulator System, or RMS for short. It was built in Canada, and it's the big brother to the robot arms on the space shuttles. The cool thing about the RMS on the Station is that it moves about like an inchworm. Whenever astronauts need to attach a new module, or fix something, they can bring the arm over to do the work. Kali – "Sprockets" – is going to have a blast playing with it.

Roger – If you talk to someone over the radio, and he or she says "roger," that means your message was received and understood. Unless that person's name happens to be Roger, in which case there may be some confusion. Maybe you should pick a different word for "message received." How about "melvin?"

Solar Array – The ISS needs a lot of electricity to power its computers, life support systems, and Yuri's video games. Since there isn't an extension cord long enough to reach from Earth, one way to generate power is to use solar energy. The arrays are designed to take sunlight and convert it into electrical current. Large batteries power the Station when it is not in sunlight.

Space Particles – Space particles are bits of rock and dust that break off of comets and asteroids. These particles can damage the ISS and the astronauts' space suits. Space particles are often called meteoroids. When they enter the Earth's atmosphere and catch fire, they're called meteors. The small parts of meteors that didn't burn up and land on the ground are called meteorites. Did you get all that? Good.

Yuri – Gizmo Yuri is named after the famous Russian cosmonaut, Yuri Gagarin. On April 12, 1961, Gagarin blasted off into space and circled the Earth one time, becoming the first person in space, and the first person to orbit the Earth. (Yep, he was the first guy to know for sure that the Earth was round.)

Published by Favorite Uncle Books, LLC,
23228 Lawrence, Dearborn, Michigan, 48128-1230.
www.FavoriteUncleBooks.com

Story by John Tocco and Douglas Tocco

Text, illustrations and Gizmo script copyright © 2003
John V. Tocco and Douglas Tocco

Cover, book design and additional words by Douglas Tocco,
www.NotionDynamics.com

3D construction courtesy of Notion Pictures, LLC,
Washington, Michigan, www.NotionPictures.com

Gizmovision.com powered by E3ID, Waterford, Michigan,
www.E3ID.com

Editorial review by Manuscript Makeovers of Springdale,
Arkansas, www.ManuscriptMakeovers.com.

Book printed and bound in Canada by Friesens Corporation,
through Four Colour Imports, Ltd., Louisville, Kentucky,
www.Friesens.com

ISBN: 0-9711665-2-8
Library of Congress Control Number: 2002096724

Special Thanks

We'd like to acknowledge the following people and organizations for their kind assistance in the creation of this book:

Staff of the Alexander Macomb
Academy, Mt. Clemens, Michigan
  Ann Tocco
  Jill Ellis
  Kerri Gipson
  Donna Schultz
  Tamara Panetta

Media Specialists of Farmington,
Michigan Public Schools
  Addie Levine
  Marilyn Hersh
  Shirley Witgen
  Carole Kirsten
  Marian Paroo

Staff of Gretchko Elementary School,
West Bloomfield, Michigan
  Kimberly Daniels
  Pamela Neubacher

The National Aeronautical
and Space Administration

Deb Tocco
Carl England
Joann Aloe
Susan Turner
Beth Michel
Monica Beil
Wendy French

Teachers/Parents/Homeschoolers

If you wish to obtain additional teaching materials, please visit www.FavoriteUncleBooks.com and www.Gizmovision.com. If you have any questions or comments regarding this book, please click on the Suggestion Box at www.FavoriteUncleBooks.com. We'd love to hear from you.

International Space Station Notes

The ISS depicted in *Meet the Gizmos* is a simplified version of the actual station. We felt it would be easier for young readers to understand. As of the publishing date of this book, the ISS has not been completed. Some components used in our version will be added to the actual Station over the next few years. For more information on the ISS or other space-related subjects, please visit www.Gizmovision.com, and click on the Launch Pad for links to NASA and other space sites.